Welcome to
Saddleback's *Illustrated Classics*

We are proud to welcome you to Saddleback's *Illustrated Classics*. Saddleback's *Illustrated Classics* was designed specifically for the classroom to introduce readers to many of the great classics in literature. Each text, written and adapted by teachers and researchers, has been edited using the Dale-Chall vocabulary system. In addition, much time and effort has been spent to ensure that these high-interest stories retain all of the excitement, intrigue, and adventure of the original books.

With these graphically *Illustrated Classics*, you learn what happens in the story in a number of different ways. One way is by reading the words a character says. Another way is by looking at the drawings of the character. The artist can tell you what kind of person a character is and what he or she is thinking or feeling.

This series will help you to develop confidence and a sense of accomplishment as you finish each novel. The stories in Saddleback's *Illustrated Classics* are fun to read. And remember, fun motivates!

Overview

Everyone deserves to read the best literature our language has to offer. Saddleback's *Illustrated Classics* was designed to acquaint readers with the most famous stories from the world's greatest authors, while teaching essential skills. You will learn how to:

- Establish a purpose for reading
- Activate prior knowledge
- Evaluate your reading
- Listen to the language as it is written
- Extend literary and language appreciation through discussion and writing activities.

Reading is one of the most important skills you will ever learn. It provides the key to all kinds of information. By reading the *Illustrated Classics*, you will develop confidence and the self-satisfaction that comes from accomplishment—a solid foundation for any reader.

Moby Dick

Herman Melville

Saddleback's *Illustrated Classics*

SADDLEBACK
EDUCATIONAL PUBLISHING
www.sdlback.com

ISBN-13: 978-1-56254-924-4
ISBN-10: 1-56254-924-3
eBook: 978-1-60291-161-1

Printed in Malaysia

21 20 19 18 17   6 7 8 9 10

Step-By-Step

The following is a simple guide to using and enjoying each of your *Illustrated Classics*. To maximize your use of the learning activities provided, we suggest that you follow these steps:

1. ***Listen!*** We suggest that you listen to the read-along. (At this time, please ignore the beeps.) You will enjoy this wonderfully dramatized presentation.

2. ***Post-reading Activities.*** You have successfully read the story and listened to the audio presentation. Now answer the multiple-choice questions and other activities in the Study Guide.

Remember,

"Today's readers are tomorrow's leaders."

Herman Melville

Herman Melville was born in 1819. His formal education ended in 1834 at age fifteen. For a time he was both clerk and school teacher, but the sea was his first love. He became a cabin boy on a merchant ship bound for England. Later, in 1841, Melville joined the crew of a whaling ship, the Acushnet, where he learned much of the background for *Moby Dick*.

Melville was influenced by the writing of Nathaniel Hawthorne and dedicated *Moby Dick* to him. Melville felt that Hawthorne had an insight into human nature that few could surpass.

Melville, too, knew mankind mainly from living in many cultures. His life with the Taipis, cannibal natives, led him to write *Typee*. From a mutiny he experienced, he wrote *Omoo*. One of his later books, and most heartrending, is *Billy Budd*—the story of a young and severely abused seaman.

In spite of his unusual creative ability, Melville spent nineteen years of his life as a customs officer in the ports of New York City. Not until after his death was he truly appreciated as an author. Today, *Moby Dick* is considered to be one of the greatest, if not the greatest, American novels.

Herman Melville

Moby Dick

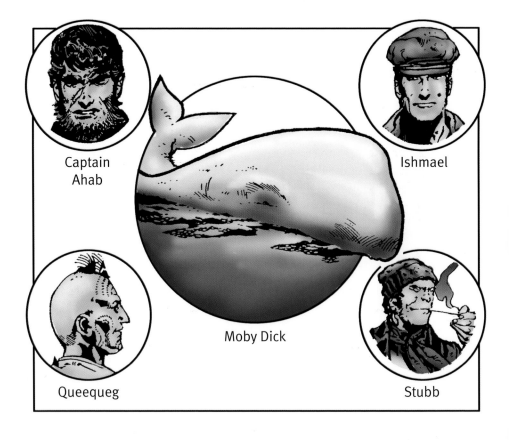

Captain
Ahab

Ishmael

Moby Dick

Queequeg

Stubb

Call me Ishmael.

Some years ago, with nothing to interest me on shore, I thought I would sail about a little and see the oceans of the world. I loved to sail dangerous seas and land on foreign coasts. I had already made a number of voyages on trading ships and now set out to go whaling. I had no idea I would meet the mad Captain Ahab and hunt for the great white whale which men called Moby Dick.

I landed in New Bedford on a Saturday night in December. I was very unhappy to learn that the boat for Nantucket had already sailed. There was no way of reaching Nantucket until Monday.

What a bitter night! I must find somewhere to stay.

I soon came to an inn.

Spouter? Coffin! Rather evil sounding—but I'll risk it.

Inside, I found the landlord.

My house is full. But wait! You have no objection to sharing a bed with a harpooner, have you?

I'll share with any good man, rather than walk about on so bitter a night.

All right. Take a seat. You want supper?

Where is that harpooner? Is he here?

He'll be here before long.

But at twelve o'clock the harpooner still hadn't come in.

Landlord! Does he always keep such late hours?

No, but tonight he went out selling, and maybe he can't sell his head.

His head?

It's just a shrunken head...a strange thing, you know... but it's getting very late. You'd better be turning in.

I took the landlord's advice. But I had not been asleep long before I awakened and...

Lord save me! The harpooner!

First he prayed to a stone god. Then, undressing, he lit up a tomahawk which he used as a pipe.

Putting out the lamp, he jumped into bed.

Who-ee devil you? Speak or I kill!

Landlord, save me!

Why didn't you tell me he was a wild man?

Don't be afraid. Queequeg wouldn't harm a hair of your head.

After some thought...

Why be upset? He's a human being, just as I am...and a whaling man. Better to sleep with a sober wild man than a drunken Christian.

If you'll just put that tomahawk away, or pipe, or whatever it is.

Me do... you get in.

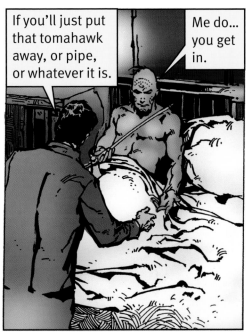

I never slept better in my life. Next morning, we had breakfast.

No coffee and rolls for him...only beefsteaks, rare.

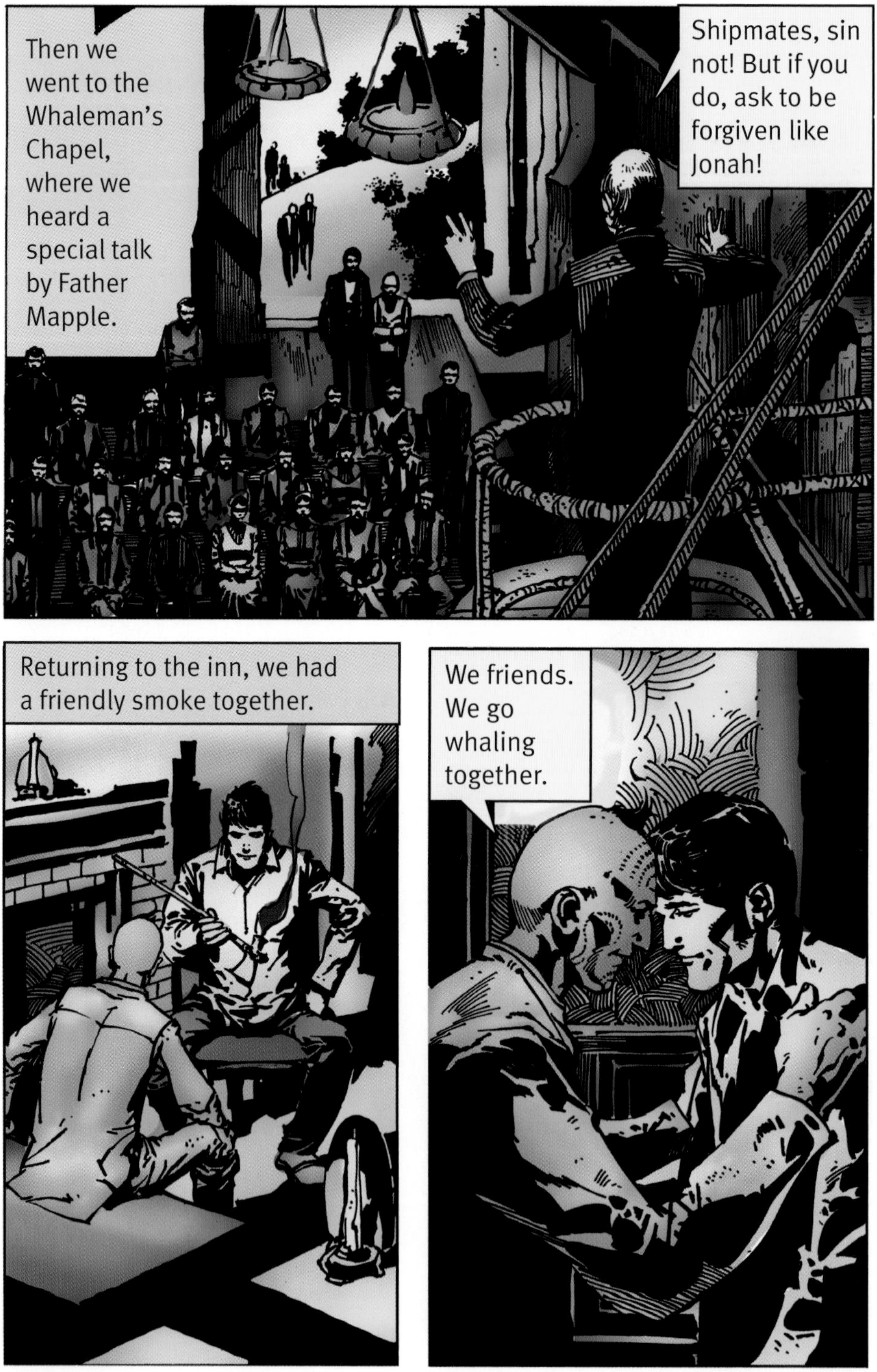
Then we went to the Whaleman's Chapel, where we heard a special talk by Father Mapple.
Shipmates, sin not! But if you do, ask to be forgiven like Jonah!
Returning to the inn, we had a friendly smoke together.
We friends. We go whaling together.

And so, on Monday, we took the boat to Nantucket.

In Nantucket, Queequeg asked his stone god, Yojo, for help.

Yojo say you find-ee ship for us.

And so I set out among the many ships. Of the ships in port, I picked the Pequod. On deck, in a tent supported by whale bone, I found Captain Peleg, a Quaker and owner of one of the boats.

Sir, I was thinking of going on a ship.

You were? What takes you a-whaling?

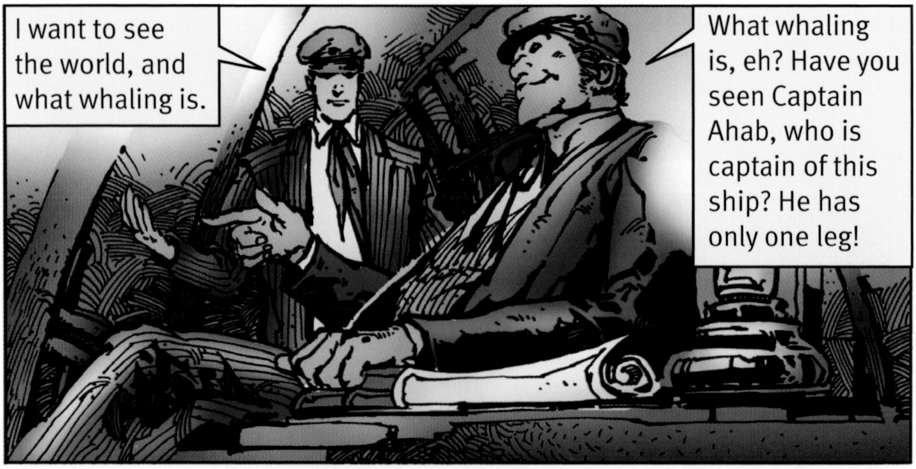
I want to see the world, and what whaling is.
What whaling is, eh? Have you seen Captain Ahab, who is captain of this ship? He has only one leg!

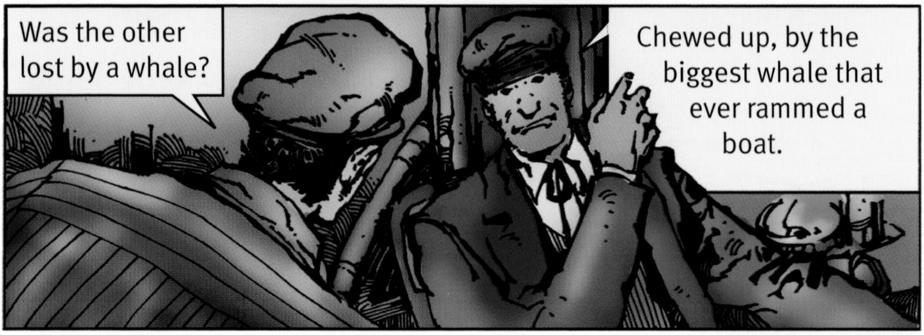
Was the other lost by a whale?
Chewed up, by the biggest whale that ever rammed a boat.

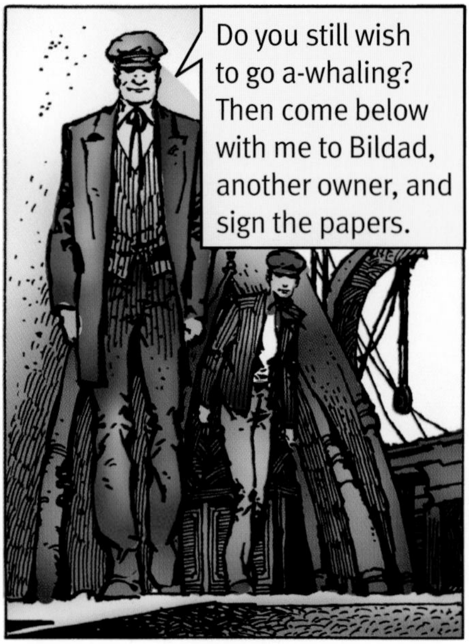
Do you still wish to go a-whaling? Then come below with me to Bildad, another owner, and sign the papers.

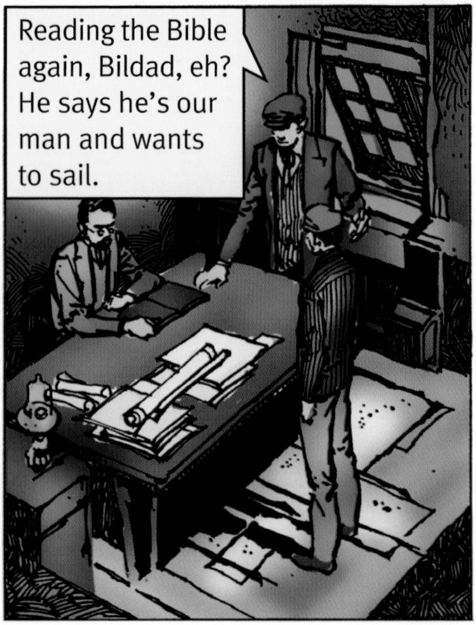
Reading the Bible again, Bildad, eh? He says he's our man and wants to sail.

Do you?

I do.

He'll do. But don't be too generous with the pay. Our duty is to the other owners of this ship, many of them widows and orphans.

Blast ye, Bildad. I'll not cheat this young man!

I have a friend who wants to sail, too. He has killed more whales than I can count.

Bring him along, then.

And so, the next day...

What a harpoon he's got! I say Quohog, or whatever your name is, did you ever spear a fish?

Queequeg jumped into a whale-boat hanging at the side.

You see small drop of tar on water. Suppose it whale eye. Watch then!

If him whale eye—why, the whale is dead!

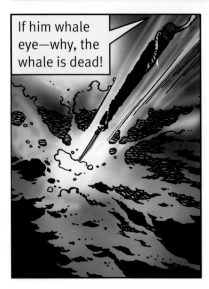

Quick, Bildad, get the ship's papers! We must have Hedgehog there, I mean Quohog! And we'll give him more than ever was given a harpooner out of Nantucket!

As we left the ship we met an old sailor.

Have you signed up with that ship? And have you seen Captain Ahab?

Ha! Captain Ahab is all right, then this left arm of mine will be all right, not before!

We haven't. They say he's sick but will soon be all right.

Come Queequeg... this fellow is crazy.

Morning to you, shipmates...and God pity you! God pity you!

For several days we were very busy on the Pequod. Supplies for three years' voyage were brought on board the ship.

Then, on a cold Christmas day we sailed, with Bildad and Peleg to lead us out of the port.

Man the anchor! Blood and thunder...jump!

Move it, you men! Pull and lift it, you men. Heave, thou Quohog!

At last Peleg and Bildad said their good-byes and got into the pilot boat. Ship and boat moved in different directions, and we sailed into the wide Atlantic, not knowing what waited for us out there.

We were a crew from many countries.

Our officers were Chief Mate Starbuck—tall, and careful...

Happy-go-lucky Stubb, the Second Mate...

And Flask, the Third Mate, who lived to kill.

But for several days nothing was seen of Captain Ahab.

What kind of man is our captain I wonder?

A man like any other. I hear he has a wife and child in Nantucket.

He is no common man, from what I hear. Something in him is bothering him and makes him do strange things.

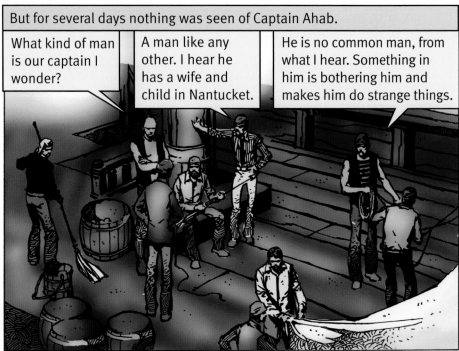

Then one day, I saw him on the quarter-deck. Something about him made me afraid.

Aye, he's frightful enough...as if filled with a great problem.

You men on top of the mastheads, there! Look sharp... there are whales around here! If you see a white one, yell the signal.

A white whale? ...there's something special in the wind, something strange!

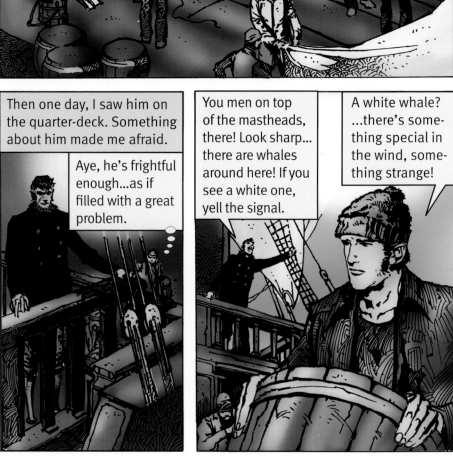

Not long after, Ahab gave an order usually only for emergencies...

Send everybody to the rear!

Sir? Yes, sir, everybody to the rear.

The entire ship's company came together.

You have heard me give orders about a white whale. Look you! Do you see this coin of gold?

He nailed the coin to the main mast.

Whosoever of you spots me a white whale with a wrinkled brow and a crooked jaw...he shall have this gold, boys!

That white whale must be the one some call Moby Dick!

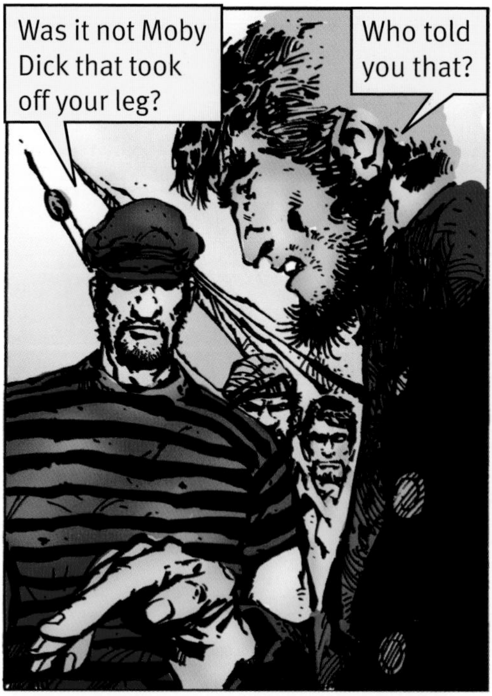
Was it not Moby Dick that took off your leg?
Who told you that?

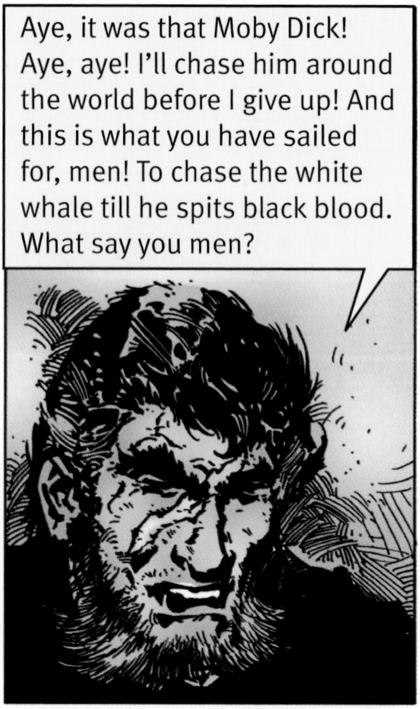
Aye, it was that Moby Dick! Aye, aye! I'll chase him around the world before I give up! And this is what you have sailed for, men! To chase the white whale till he spits black blood. What say you men?

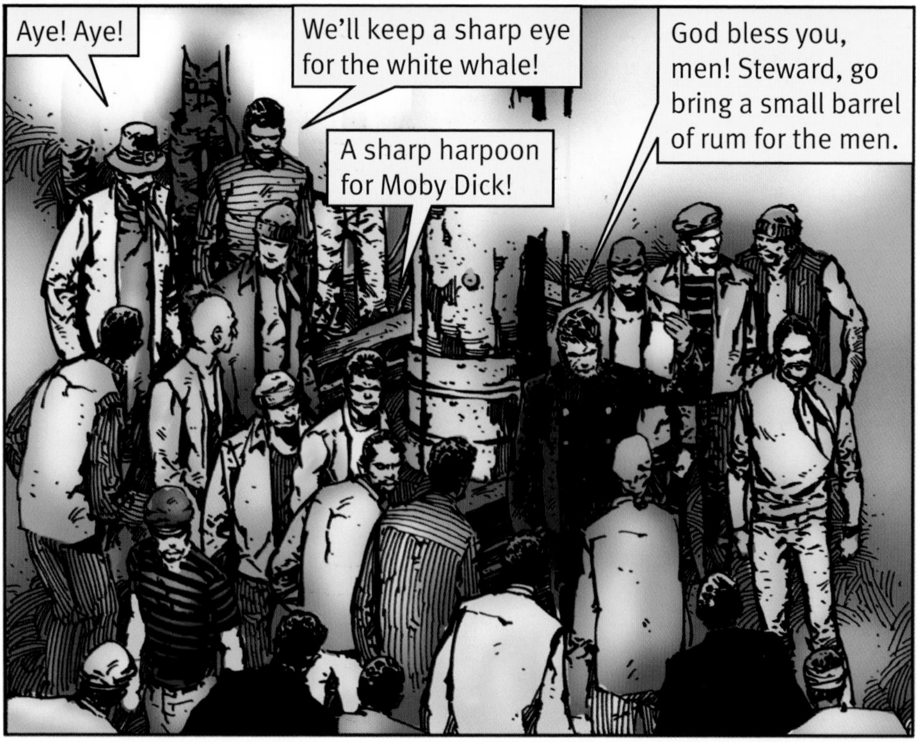
Aye! Aye!
We'll keep a sharp eye for the white whale!
A sharp harpoon for Moby Dick!
God bless you, men! Steward, go bring a small barrel of rum for the men.

Aren't you going after Moby Dick, Mr. Starbuck?

I am brave enough, Captain. But I came to hunt whales, not my captain's vengeance. How many barrels of oil will it give? What will it bring on the market?

A curse on a dumb bully of an animal struck without knowing what he did! Madness! It goes against God.

Don't talk to me of God, man! I'd strike the sun if it insulted me! Some strange unknown power struck at me though the whale... shall I not strike back?

Ah, the barrel of rum! Drink men, and pass it on!

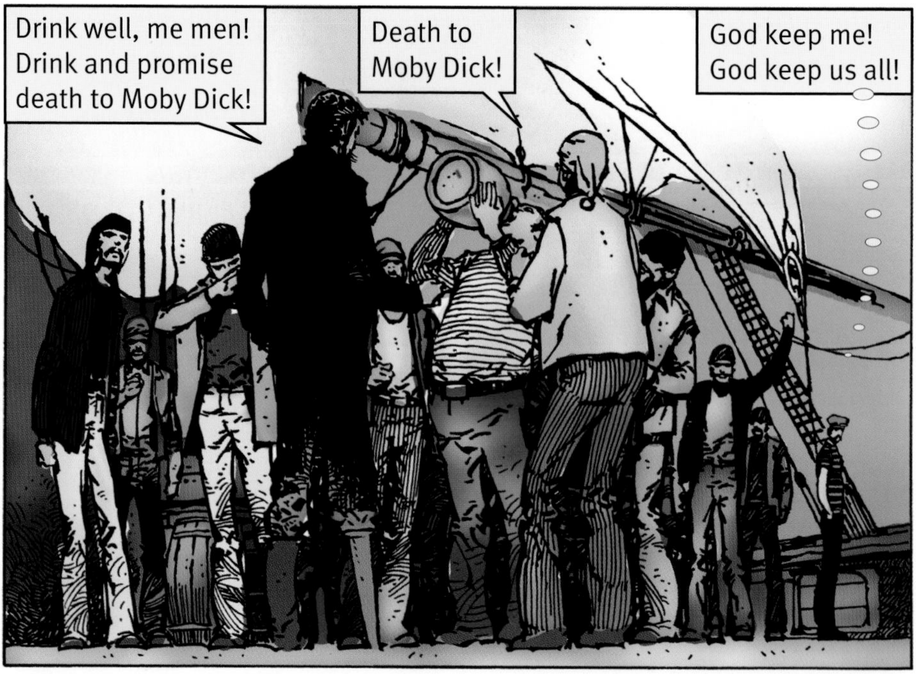
Drink well, me men! Drink and promise death to Moby Dick!
Death to Moby Dick!
God keep me! God keep us all!

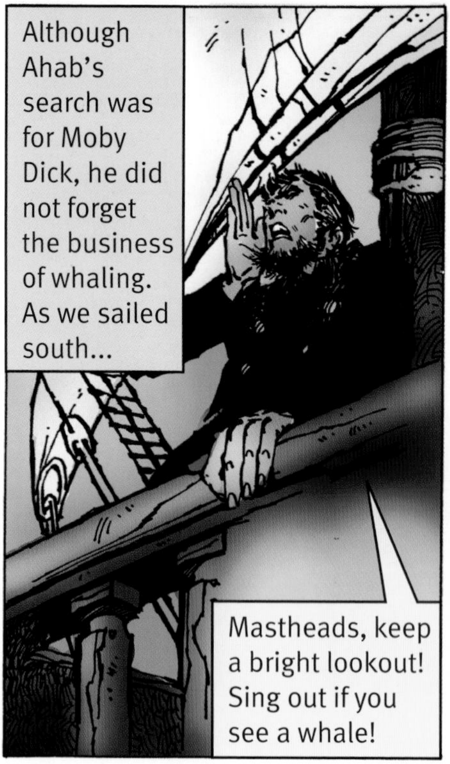
Although Ahab's search was for Moby Dick, he did not forget the business of whaling. As we sailed south...
Mastheads, keep a bright lookout! Sing out if you see a whale!

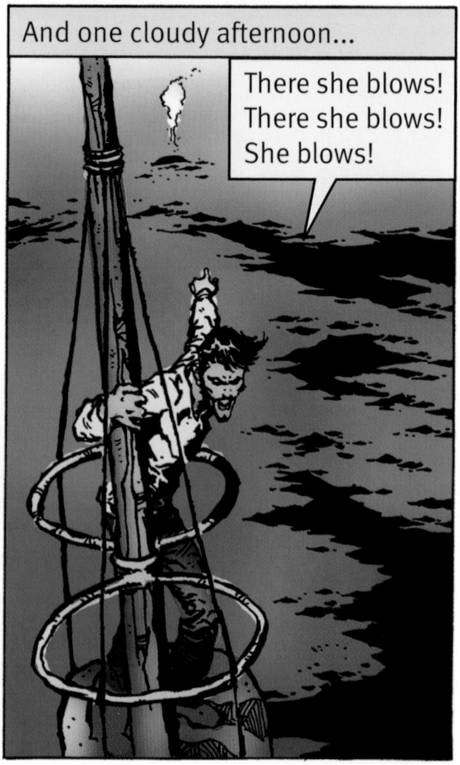
And one cloudy afternoon...
There she blows! There she blows! She blows!

The order to lower the boats into the water was given and we set out to find the whale.

I was in Starbuck's boat and soon...

Row, boys, row! There's a storm coming, but we've still time to kill a whale!

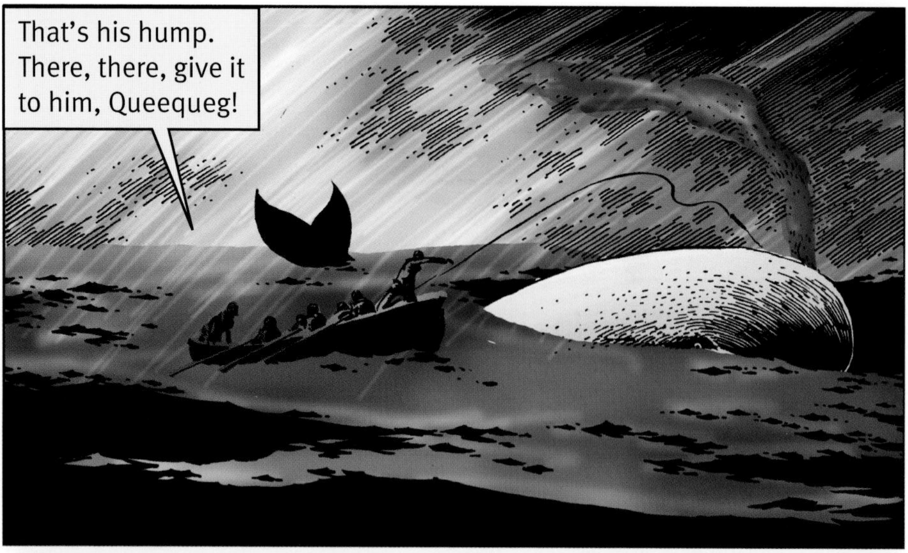
That's his hump. There, there, give it to him, Queequeg!

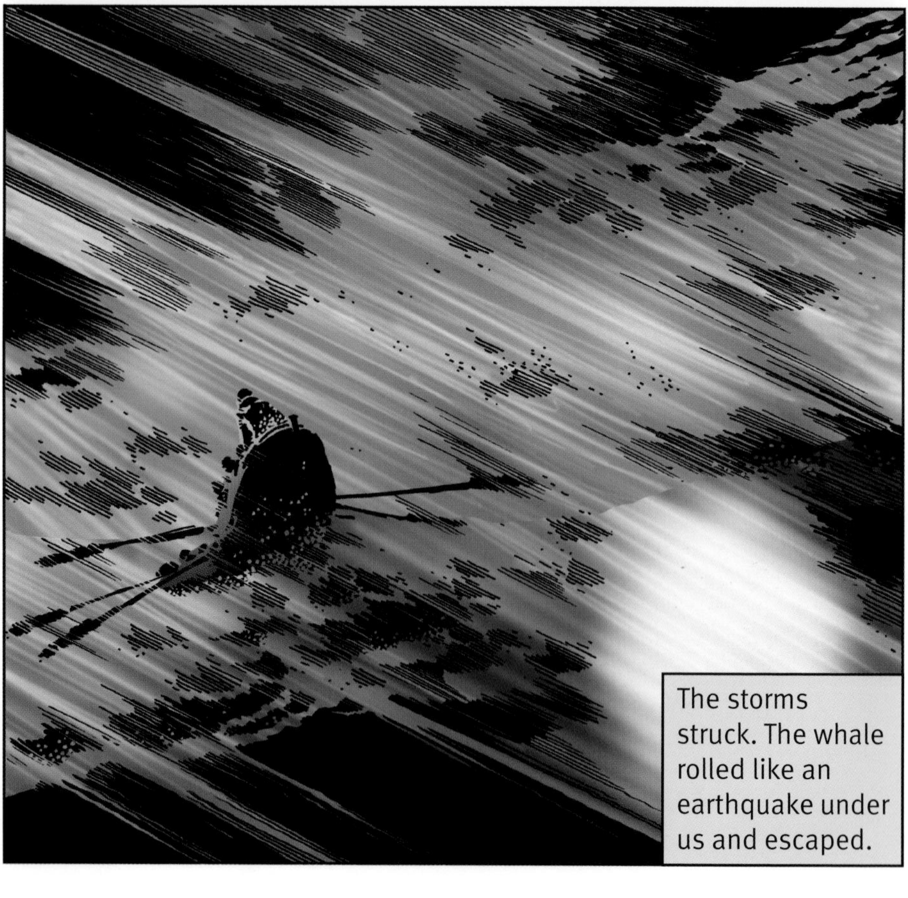
The storms struck. The whale rolled like an earthquake under us and escaped.

All night we floated in our water-filled boat...

At dawn...

Look out men! Jump!

Our own ship had hit us in the dark but we were quickly rescued.

But there were other days, and other whales. On one chase, Stubb's boat led the rest.

Give it to him, Tashtego!

Changing places with the harpooner, Stubb dug his spear into the whale.

The whale went into its flurry, churning the water...

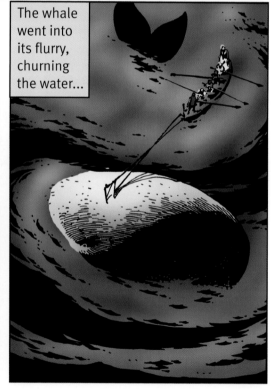

Until...

He's dead, Mr. Stubb.

Yes, he's stopped blowing water.

The whale was pulled to the ship.

Then the men tied it to the side of the Pequod with chains.

The head was cut off and dropped over the back of the ship, where it was held by a chain.

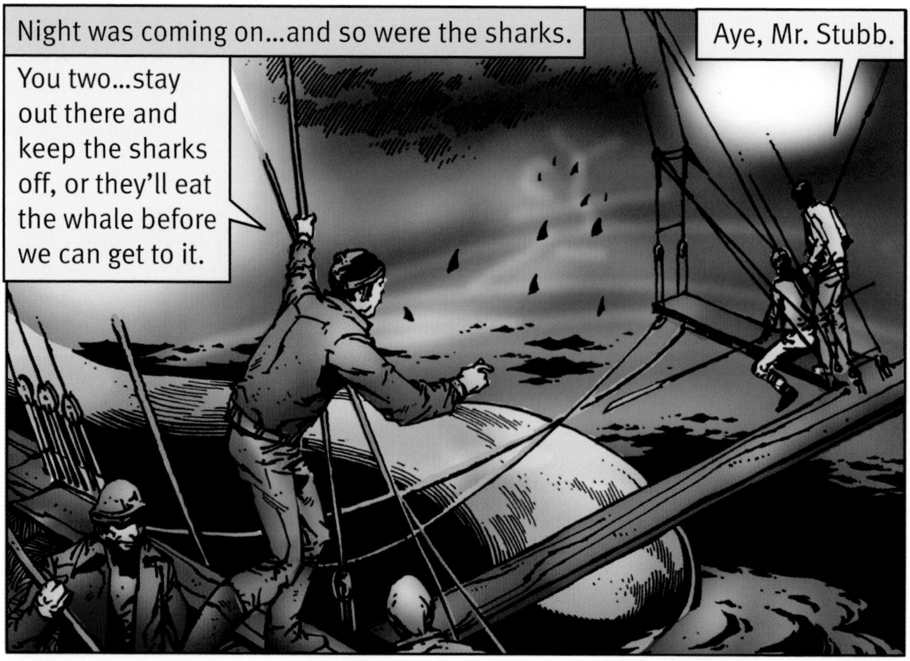
Night was coming on...and so were the sharks.
Aye, Mr. Stubb.
You two...stay out there and keep the sharks off, or they'll eat the whale before we can get to it.

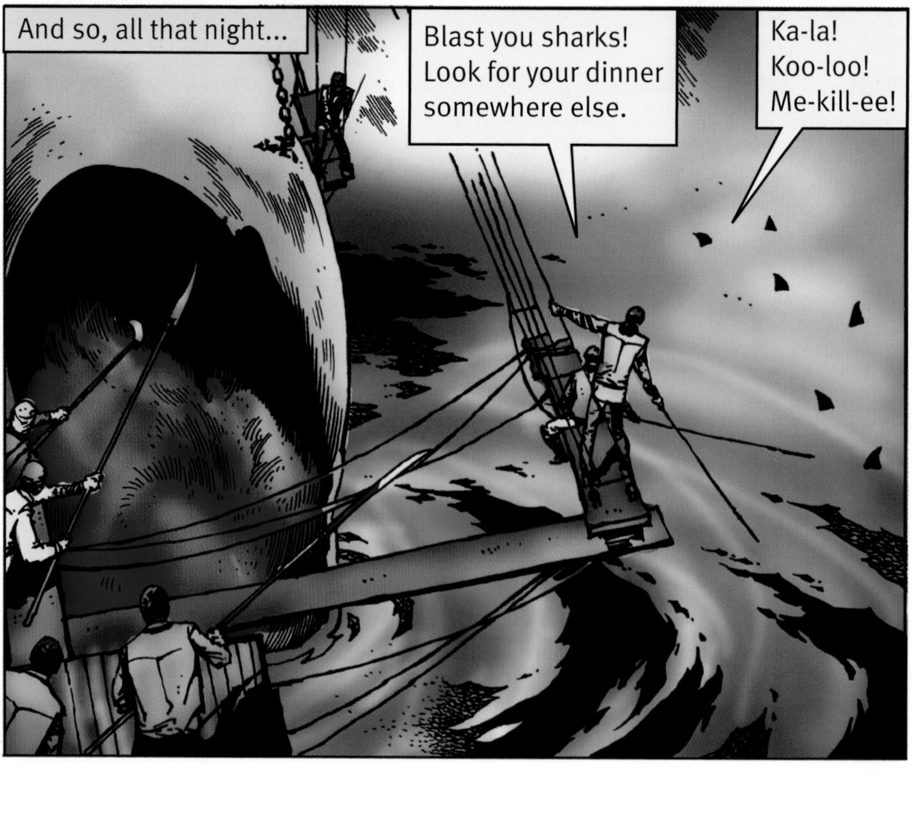
And so, all that night...
Blast you sharks! Look for your dinner somewhere else.
Ka-la! Koo-loo! Me-kill-ee!

Next day, with hook and chain, the blubber was cut from the whale.

The peeled white body was cut loose and drifted away.

What a sad funeral for such a mighty animal!

The blubber was cut into smaller pieces!

Then the blubber was boiled down into oil in a large pot.

At night, in the darkness, the ship seemed to be on fire.

In the morning the whale's head was pulled up so that the very valuable oil called spermaceti could be taken from a case inside the head.

Tashtego climbed on top of the head and dug a hole with a sharp spade.

He pushed a bucket into the hole with a long pole.

Time and again the bucket was lifted up to the deck, where the oil was emptied into a tub.

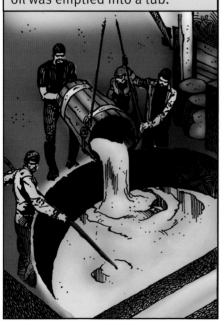

Then...a slip of the foot...and...

H-help!

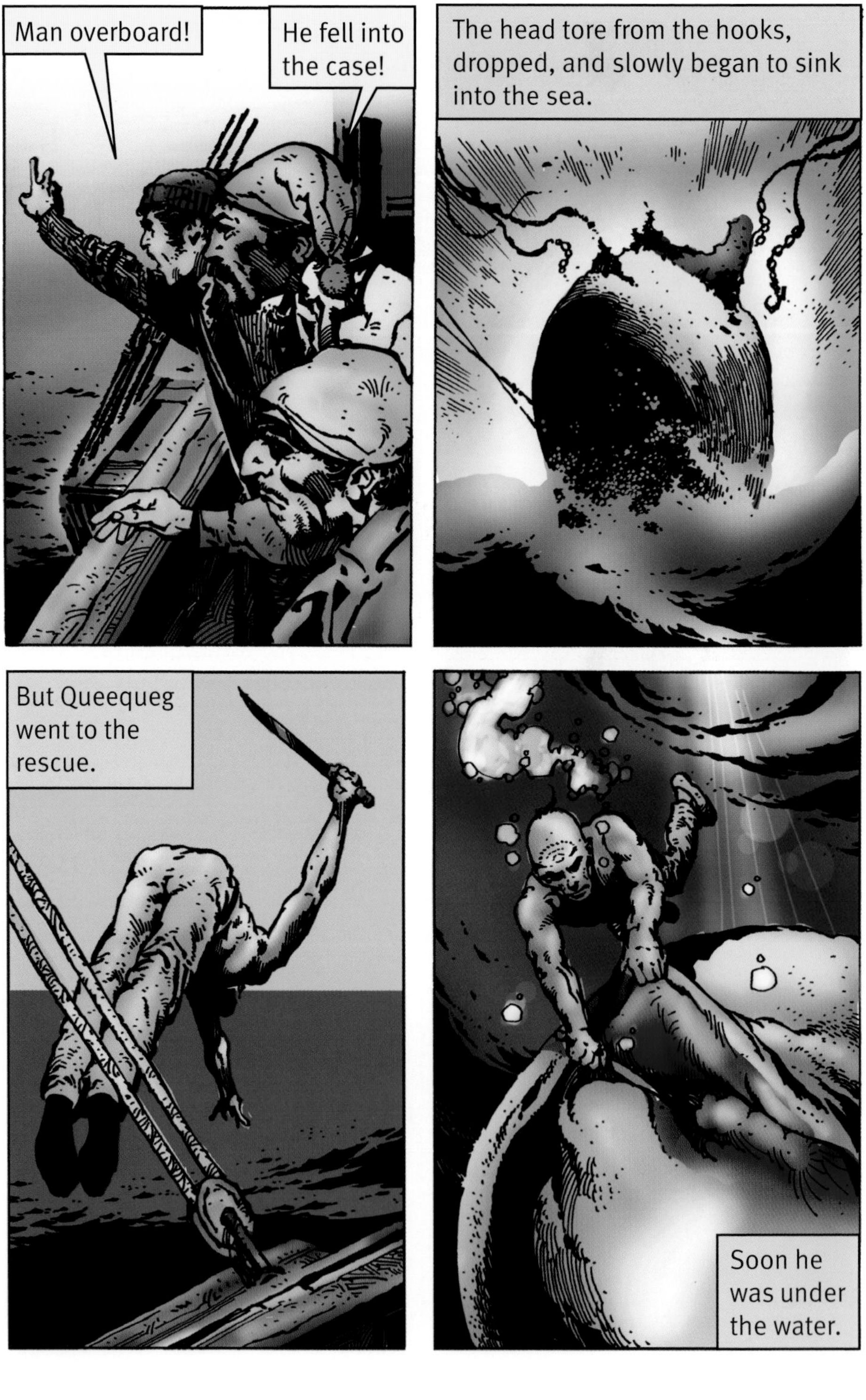
Man overboard!
He fell into the case!
The head tore from the hooks, dropped, and slowly began to sink into the sea.
But Queequeg went to the rescue.
Soon he was under the water.

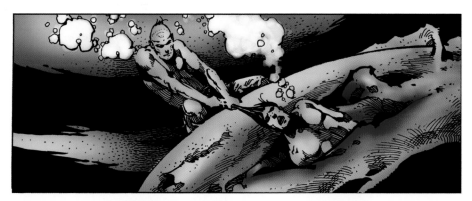

In a few moments....

Look, he's got him!

Many a whale did we catch as we sailed southward, but Ahab had only one thought.

We near Japan...these are the waters where Moby Dick may hide.

He heard a footstep at the door, and...

Who's there?

It is I, Starbuck, Captain Ahab.

Sir, oil is leaking from some barrels in the hold. We must stop and...

What? Stop here for a week to repair old barrels.

If we do not, we will waste more oil in a day than we may get in a year. What will the owners say?

Owners? What do I care about the owners. Go on deck!

A better man than I might well pass over in you what he would resent in a young man. Aye, and in a happier man, too.

Do you dare to think wrongly of me? Get on deck!

Grabbing a loaded gun, Ahab aimed at Starbuck.

There is one God that is Lord over the earth, and one captain that is Lord over the Pequod. Now I order you to get on deck.

You have made me angry, sir, but you don't have to fear Starbuck. But Ahab should fear Ahab. Beware of yourself, old man.

What's that he said? Ahab, beware of Ahab... there's something true about what he says.

A little later on the deck...

You are too good a fellow, Starbuck. Head for land and repair the barrel.

After the barrels were repaired the Pequod sailed on, and....

Blacksmith, make me a spear...one that will stick in a whale like his own fin-bone.

Is this harpoon for the white whale, sir?

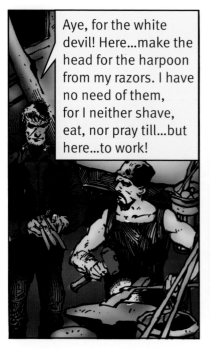

Aye, for the white devil! Here...make the head for the harpoon from my razors. I have no need of them, for I neither shave, eat, nor pray till...but here...to work!

Ahab made the harpoon ready, not in water, but in blood drawn from the harpooners.

I baptize thee not in the name of the Father, but in the name of the devil!

As we sailed in the Japan seas, a storm broke on us from a cloudless sky.

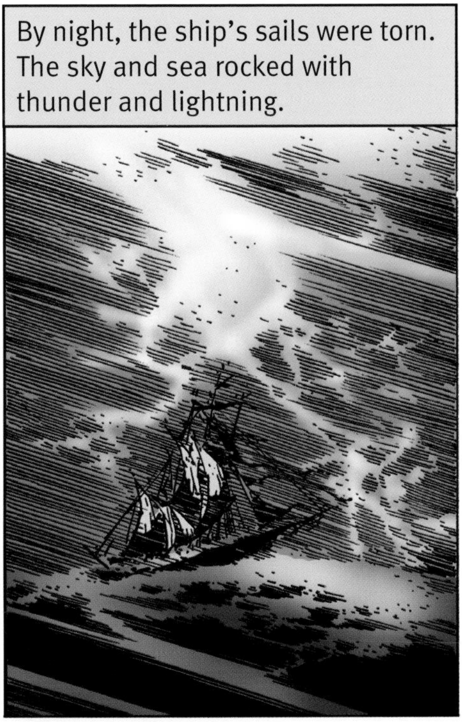
By night, the ship's sails were torn. The sky and sea rocked with thunder and lightning.

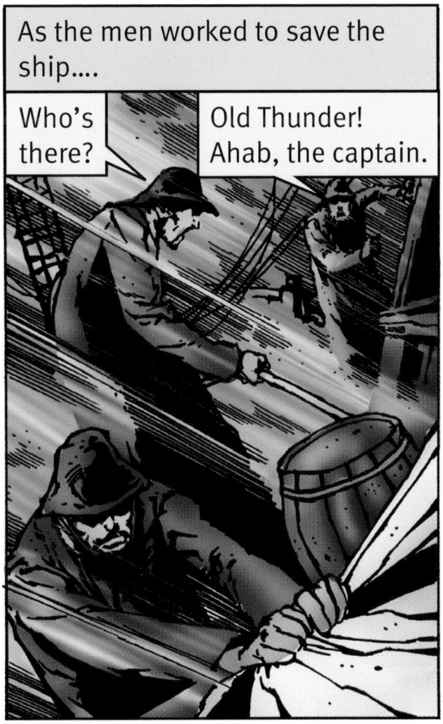
As the men worked to save the ship....
Who's there?
Old Thunder! Ahab, the captain.

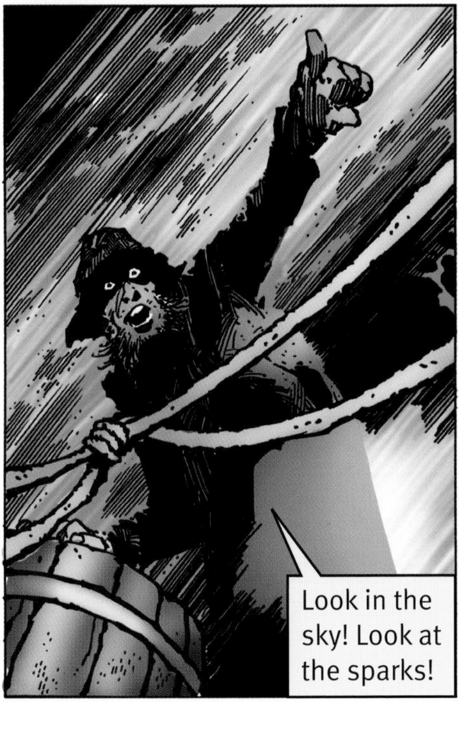
Look in the sky! Look at the sparks!

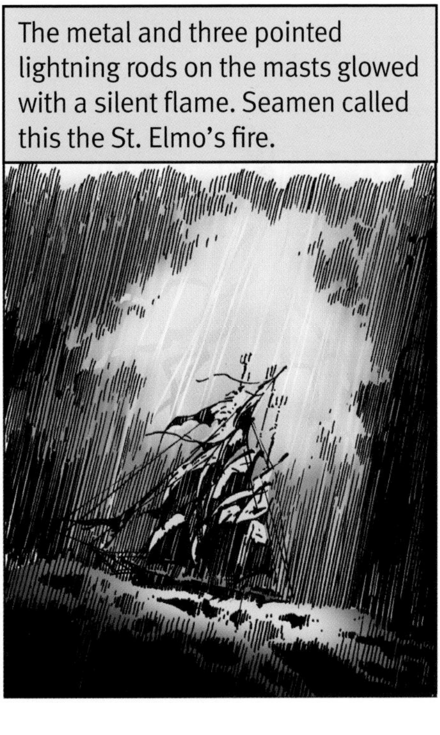
The metal and three pointed lightning rods on the masts glowed with a silent flame. Seamen called this the St. Elmo's fire.

Although the men had all seen this kind of thing before, they watched, frozen in their shoes.

God have mercy on us all!

It almost lights the way to the white whale!

Ahab held the chain of the main-mast lightning rod.

I will pretend to feel the pulse, and let mine beat against it...blood against fire! Leap up, fire! I leap with thee, worship thee!

Thy harpoon, captain! It glows with a ball of fire!

God is against thee, old man! This voyage will end in no good. Turn back!

Aye, let us sail home while we may!

But Ahab held the burning harpoon!

All of you promised to hunt for the white whale with me. We will all hunt, do you hear! Look here...

With one breath he blew out the flame.

Thus I blow out the last fear!

The storm ended, and some hours later Starbuck went to Ahab's cabin to report that new sails had been put up and the ship was again on course.

He sleeps within. Shall I wake him...to drag us all to our doom?

He would have shot me...with this very gun!

Shall I let this crazy old man bring us all to our death? Would I be a murderer if...if...

Then within the stateroom, Ahab cried out in his sleep.

Stern all! Oh, Moby Dick, I hold your heart at last!

No...no, I cannot...even though any day I may sink with all the crew to the bottom of the sea.

Sailing on, the Pequod met the Rachel, another whaler from Nantucket.

Have you seen the white whale?

Aye, yesterday.

The captain of the Rachel came aboard the Pequod.

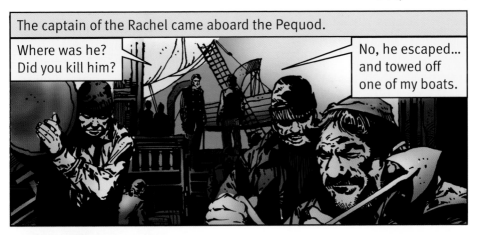

Where was he? Did you kill him?

No, he escaped... and towed off one of my boats.

My boy...my own boy...was on that boat. Won't you help me find it?

His son lost! We must save that boy.

Let me rent your ship for forty-eight hours! I'll pay and pay well! You have a child of your own safely at home...you must understand...you must help!

I will not do it. Even now I lose time. Good-bye and God bless you man, but I must go after Moby Dick.

The captain went back to the Rachel to continue the search. We watched her as we sailed swiftly away....

They haven't found the lost boy...I doubt they ever will.

A few days later...

Moby Dick is around here. I must have the first sight of him myself! Make me a seat and raise me to the masthead!

From his high seat on top of the mast, Ahab watched the sea.

Show yourself, you monster! Ahab challenges Moby Dick!

Not long after...

A mild day, Starbuck. On such a sweet day I struck my first whale... forty years ago. Out of those forty years I have not spent three ashore. I have grown old and tired on the uncaring sea!

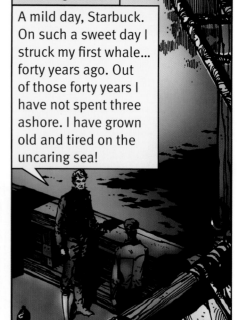

So little time have I spent on land... my wife's been alone since I wed her. What a forty years' fool has old Ahab been!

In your eyes, as in a magic glass, I see my home...and yours! Stay aboard the Pequod when Ahab gives chase to Moby Dick! The danger shall not be yours. You shall live to see home again!

Oh, my captain! Give up the chase of that hated monster! Let us turn back, and you, too, shall see home again!

Some nameless thing keeps me here. Some hidden lord and master drives me on...I dare not turn back.

Silently, without hope, Starbuck slipped away.

48

That night, Ahab suddenly smelled the sea air....

That strange odor...it's a whale! Moby Dick is near!

Next morning, he ordered all hands on deck.

See you nothing? No sign of the white whale? Pull me aloft!

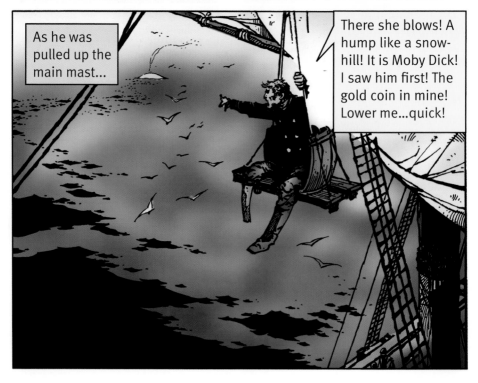

As he was pulled up the main mast...

There she blows! A hump like a snow-hill! It is Moby Dick! I saw him first! The gold coin in mine! Lower me...quick!

Soon...

Lower the boats!
Boats, boats!
Mr. Starbuck,
remember,
stay on board
the ship!

As the boats raced toward the monster...

There! He sounds!

Changing places, Ahab went to the bow and looked down.

I see his open jaw just below! Stand close to the stern!

The whale swam upwards, turning on its back, and...

Look out, captain!

His jaws slowly closed on the boat...but one of his teeth caught on an oarlock.

Ahab grabbed the long tooth trying to work it free.

Blast it, to hold me helpless in your very jaws.

Suddenly the jaws slipped from him, and...

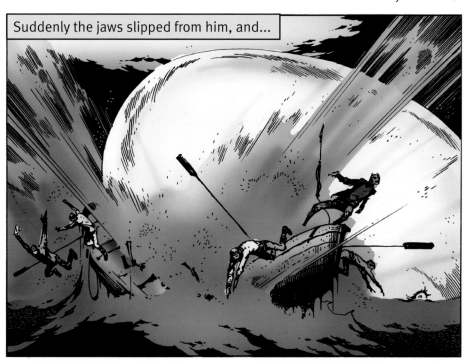

The whale caused the water to turn so that Ahab barely kept above it.

Then the Pequod, which had been standing by, sailed up.

Sail on the whale! Drive him away!

The whale was driven off, and the boats flew to the rescue.

Next day, Ahab again sighted the whale.

There she blows! There she blows in the waves!

Look for the last time at the sun, Moby Dick! Thy hour and thy harpoon are at hand!

In a few moments...

Lower the boats! Mr. Starbuck, stay aboard and look after the ship!

This time the whale rushed at the boats...

...then dashed his head against the bottom of Ahab's boat.

Again the Pequod rescued the men and boats.

Let me lean on you, Starbuck...my ivory leg is broken. But I will kill the white whale yet, even if I circle the world ten times; and even dive right through it!

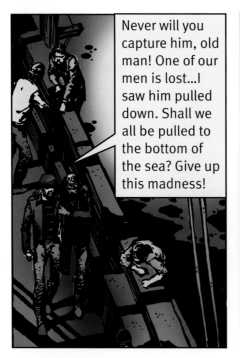

Never will you capture him, old man! One of our men is lost...I saw him pulled down. Shall we all be pulled to the bottom of the sea? Give up this madness!

Though I like you for some strange reason, you are a fool. I must go on, lieutenant! I act under orders, I must obey and chase Moby Dick! I must!

The next day the weather was clear. After an hour's watching...

There! She blows! I meet thee, this third time, Moby Dick!

Again Ahab gave the order for the chase, and...

Starbuck! For the third time my ship starts upon this voyage!

Aye, sir, you will have it.

I am old... shake hands with me, man.

Oh, my captain! Do not go! See, it's a brave man that weeps.

I go! Lower away! Stand by the crew!

As the boats started forward, Moby Dick turned the water furiously.

Rushing head on, the whale overturned two boats, but left Ahab's almost without a scar.

While the two boats were brought aboard the ship to be repaired, Ahab's boat, alone, chased the whale.

The sharks are chewing up the oars!

They will last long enough! Pull on!

With a curse, Ahab threw the harpoon.

It sank deep, but the whale pushed on, and the line snapped.

Suddenly, as the Pequod sailed up, the whale turned toward the ship.

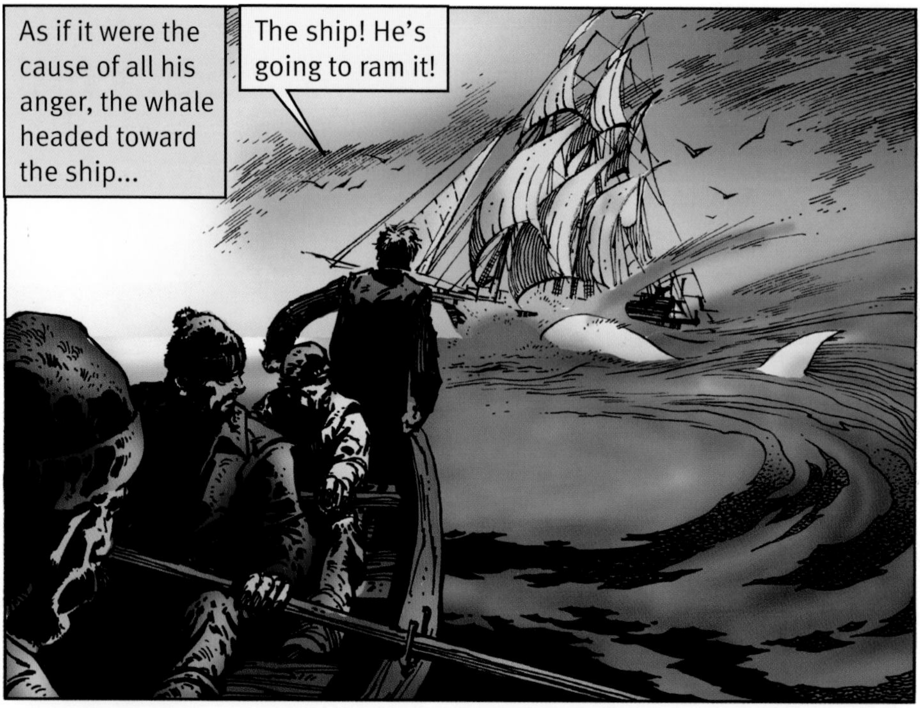
As if it were the cause of all his anger, the whale headed toward the ship...
The ship! He's going to ram it!

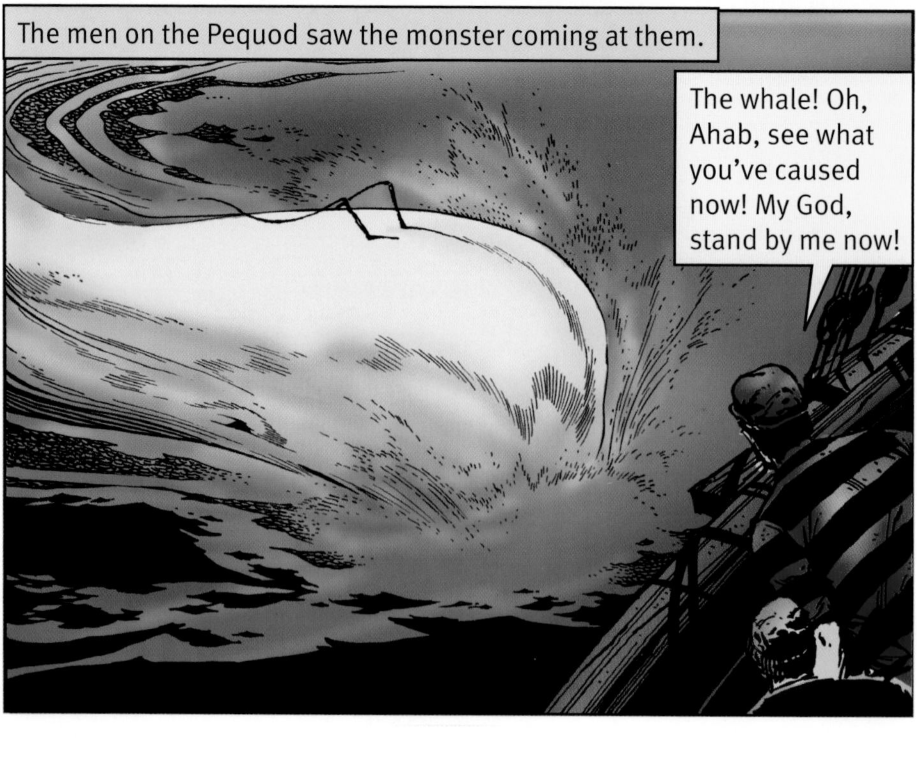
The men on the Pequod saw the monster coming at them.
The whale! Oh, Ahab, see what you've caused now! My God, stand by me now!

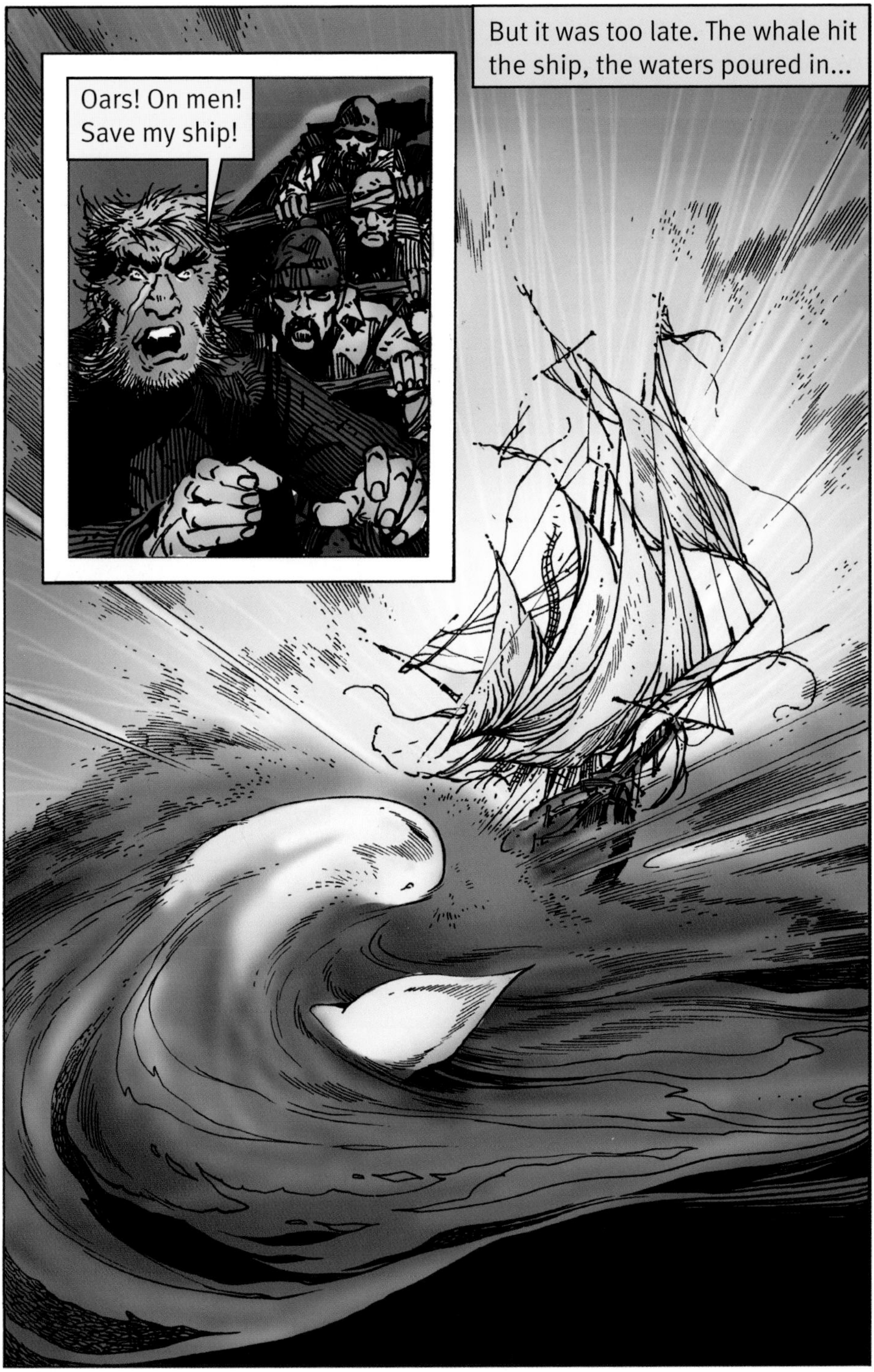
Oars! On men!
Save my ship!
But it was too late. The whale hit the ship, the waters poured in...

Death to my ship! Must she die? And without me? Am I not able to go down with my ship as is the wish of all brave captains? Oh lonely death after lonely life.

Ho! Towards you I come, you monster whale. To the end of my life I will fight with you.

From my heart I stab you; for hate's sake I spit my last breath at you! Thus I give up the spear!

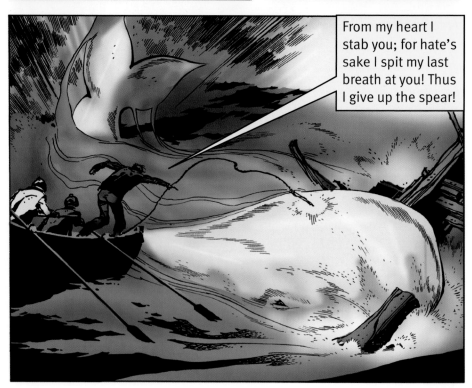

Again the harpoon struck. The whale flew forward.

The line got tangled. Ahab bent to clear it, but the flying turn caught him around the neck.

He was shot out of the boat, and disappeared into the waves.

For an instant the boat's crew stood, as though in a trance.

Great God, where is the ship?

The ship, too, was disappearing into the ocean. And now drawn by the suction of the sinking ship, the small boat and all in it, and the smallest chip of the Pequod, were carried out of sight under the waves.

Then all was finished, and the great blanket of sea rolled on as it rolled five thousand years ago.

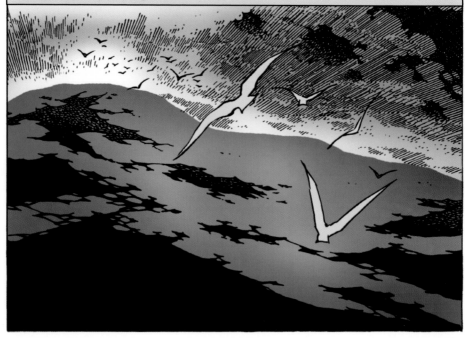

The story is done. But one did live through this wreck...I, Ishmael.

On the second day, a sail drew near. It was the Rachel, that in her search after her missing children, only found another orphan.

And I alone escaped to tell thee.

The End